For Dr. Sally

We've seen you
enough-you qualify as
an honorary "Aunt Sally"

Thanks for seeing us
to better health.

Henry i Pete
al

THE ADVENTURES OF WIKI AND THE ROCK PEOPLE

BY: BRADY STANTON

ILLUSTRATIONS BY:
PETER BRUNKE
COLOR AND DESIGN BY:
IVY HOLGATE FIFE

Library of Congress Catalog Card Number : 94-92426
ISBN 0-9643873-0-1

Published in Fairway, Kansas, by Stanton Publishing.
Manufactured in the United States of America.

For Kathryn & Duncan,
and anyone else with
a little kid left in them.

This is a tale of Wiki and the Rock People.
The Rock People are from a near away place
in a far away time.

From back when imagination
was the center of the universe.
In a land where wild Wakkas filled the skies-
flying backward and in reverse.

Where chirping bellahooples
blew bubbles in the sea,
which tickled the noses
of the Purple Ponka trees.

The Allibabba Babies
lived upon this land.
They lived in houses
made from boxes
that grew around the bend.

And in the third house,
just up on the left,
up from the singing gate-
there played a 'Babba Baby
and Wiki was his name.

He played 'neath the skies
  of two sons of Suns
that shined so bright and so warm.
  Two suns in the sky,
  one low and one high,
to chase away the storms.

At night he would dream
'neath a triangle moon
of places far away-
of mountains and dragons
and puppies and wagons
and games he liked to play.

Then one magical night
   when the moon shone so bright
   that it looked like glittering gold.
Wiki's dreams came to life,
   which was pleasantly nice,
and he travelled to Sleepville so bold.

On his way as he flew
to places he knew
he was met by a flittering Snicket.
A Snicket's a thing
that you'll find in your dreams
it's a mix of a snail and a cricket.

"Hi!" hailed the Snicket
as it bounded a thicket
and smiled in Wiki's direction.
Wiki smiled too,
as he flew and he flew,
for he knew he had
made some connection.

"Where have you come from and where will you go?"
the Snicket questioned brightly.
"I come from my house just as quick as a mouse
for reasons I don't know just rightly."

"You come for a reason.
 There's always a reason.
 You flew through the tickety-tock
 You come to behold
  what's here to be told.
 You come for the lonliest rock."

"Mr. Snicket?" he said,
   slowly scratching his head,
   "Are you sure that it's me that you seek?"

"It has to be true,
   it's undoubtedly you—
   no way it could only be maybe.
For the one who would come,
   who is second to none,
   is Wiki the Allibabba Baby."

His speedy quick flight
   came to an end
  at the base of a marvelous tree.
It was the craziest, wackiest, funniest tree
   that Wiki ever did see.

Its branches were wide
   and its bark soft as flowers.
It shook all its branches and showered
   young Wiki in a rainbow of colors.

Wiki laughed as one very large leaf
  landed upon his head.
As he reached to take it off,
  a soft low voice said.

"I am Kooka-Walla.
  I have crowned you as king of this hollow.
You are Wiki the wise-
  who has flown through the skies
    and to whom so many will follow."

"This colorful crown
   that you wear on your head
 is magical through and through.
 It will serve you just right
   on this mystical night
 for the things that you're going to do.

"What do you speak of,
and why do you say
that Wiki is here for a reason?"

"I only came here
on a whisper of air
to enjoy this beautiful season."

He got no reply,
not a grunt or a sigh,
the tree went ever so silent.

Then along came a wind,
blowing end over end
and blew him away so defiant.

Wiki was lifted from peak top to valley
and could see the rooftops below.
There was no way to beat it,
so he simply repeated "Hello, hello, hello."

His voice rang out
 like strings of a harp
until he came down
 in the arms of a Yarp.

"Hello my good Yarpling,
 good thing you were here,
or I might have landed
 quite badly I fear."

The Yarp set him down,
  with grace and with ease-
like a cherry on top of whipped cream
  if you please.

"The crown that you wear
  is so colorfully bright,
I would have seen you
  by day or by night.
Kooka-Walla has told us
  that you might come by-
and the wind brought your voice
  singing 'hello!' and 'hi!'."

"You've come just in time
there's not a moment to waste.
Don't doddle, don't tarry,
please hurry, make haste."

"A terrible thing has befallen the land,
it's something, quite simply,
we don't understand."

The Yarp's face grew long
  with each word that he spoke-
he had to stop twice
  for fear he would choke.

"It seems, good sir Wiki,"
  he continued to talk,
"We can't get a word
  from the stones or the rocks."

This was a problem,
a problem indeed,
This called for some action,
these folks were in need.

"Give me direction
and show me the way-
where are these rocks
that you speak of today?"

"They're down by the brook,"
the Yarp pointed down.
"They're down there,
You'll find them,"
he said with a frown.

Without hesitation,
Wiki took to the Trail.
He knew if he tried,
he'd somehow prevail.

He marched down the hill
to the place by the brook,
Then stopped for a moment
to take a good look.

He was tired from travelling
and about to sit down
when he looked at the rock
and he noticed a frown.

"What is your problem,
what troubles you so?
Tell me, I'm curious,
I'd just like to know."

The rock, it said nothing,
 it just sat there not moving.
So, Wiki turned to the brook
 whose sound was quite soothing.
"Mr. Brook, you've been here
 so incredibly long,
I can tell by the sound
 of your beautiful song."

"Do you have an idea,
 a notion, a clue-
the rocks have stopped talking-
 is there nothing to do?"

Now most brooks are babblers,
    They say nothing worth knowing-
they just start talking
    and keep going and going.
But this little brook,
    with its water so pure,
offered a solution,
    an answer, a cure.

"Wiki the Wise,
 if that's who you are,
you've travelled to here
 quite a ways, very far.
The rocks are still talking,
 I'll tell you, I know.
They just speak softly-
 so softly and slow."

"Is it true Mr. Rock?"
Wiki said in dismay.
"You've been talking a lot,
with good things to say?

I'll sit here with you,
I'll stay for awhile.
Tell me a story,"
Wiki said with a smile.

As the first sun came peeking
in back of the moon-
Wiki knew he must leave,
but he'd come back very soon.

He gave the rocks hugs
and a kind little pat-
and the rock gave a smile-
a big one in fact.

"Wiki the Wise-
     who talks to the stones-
next time you're here,
     use me as your throne."
Good friends are rare-
     that much I know-
but I'll be with you
     wherever you go."

The Yarp wandered down
and shrieked with delight-
"Wiki's not joking,
the rocks speak tonight!"
"Tell me, oh tell me,
sir Wiki the Wise-
How did you do it?"
he said with surprise.

Wiki patted the Yarp
as he looked in his eyes,
"you just have to listen-
that's word to the wise."

THE END